A GIFT FROM
SAINT NICHOLAS

A GIFT FROM SAINT NICHOLAS

adapted by CAROLE KISMARIC
from a story by
Felix Timmermans
with illustrations by
CHARLES MIKOLAYCAK

Holiday House/New York

Adaptation of text copyright © 1988 by Carole Kismaric
Illustrations copyright © 1988 by Charles Mikolaycak
Printed in the United States of America
First Edition

Library of Congress Cataloging-in-Publication Data

Kismaric, Carole

A gift from Saint Nicholas.
Freely adapted from an original story by Felix
Timmermans.
Summary: By the time Saint Nicholas gets to Cecile's
house on Saint Nicholas Eve he is out of presents, but
she remembers the wonderful chocolate boat in the nearby
candy shop.
[1. Saint Nicholas' Day---Fiction]   I. Mikolaycak,
Charles, ill.   II. Timmermans, Felix, 1886-1947.
Nood van Sinter-Klaas.   III. Title.
PZ7.K667Gi   1988   [E]   87-8797
ISBN 0-8234-0674-1

To Thomas Blum, who got us started.
C.K. & C.M.

Flakes of soft snow drifted from the silent sky one Saint Nicholas Eve. Everyone was sleeping soundly, knowing Saint Nicholas would arrive before morning.

But one child was still awake. Ever since Cecile had seen the chocolate boat in Trinchen Mutser's candy shop, she had dreamed about it every night. It was half a foot tall and as long as her arm. Trinchen Mutser called it the *Congo*, as it had come from very far away. Maybe, if Cecile stayed awake long enough, she would catch the boat as it sailed down the chimney, a gift from Saint Nicholas, the friend of all children.

In another part of town someone else was wide awake. Trinchen Mutser looked around The Sugared Nostril, her almost empty candy shop. She had managed to sell every gingerbread man, candy cane and chocolate-covered biscuit. Only the *Congo* was left, lonely and abandoned, puffing its cotton smoke. Where was her head when she bought it? Such an extravagant piece for her little store. The *Congo*'s puffing cotton smoke alone cost ninety groschen!

"Maybe I could sell the boat piece by piece," Trinchen Mutser mused aloud. Keeping the shop open longer than usual, she waited and waited and worried and worried. She lit a candle to Saint Anthony, another to Saint Nicholas and said a prayer that she might turn a profit with the *Congo*. When she grew too drowsy to think, she closed the curtains and went to bed.

While Trinchen Mutser slept, little Cecile waited by the fireplace. She was wishing so hard for the *Congo*, she did not notice the moon suddenly begin to beam with an intense brightness. Nor did she see the donkey, who with one man on top, and another

holding onto his tail, slid down the moonbeam as if on ice. Thus, without anyone noticing, Saint Nicholas and his assistant, Ruphrecht, had come to visit the town, carrying sacks brimming with delicious sweets.

They set to work. Saint Nicholas made his rounds up one street and down another. He visited every home in which a child lived, while Ruphrecht climbed over the roofs like a cat, dropping gifts down each chimney. Together, they left the well-behaved children sugary sweets and the real good-for-nothings a lump of coal.

"Well, we have finished our task until next year," sighed Ruphrecht, wiping his sooty face with his coat sleeve.

Saint Nicholas noticed they were near Cecile's

house. "And what about the child Cecile?" he asked.

At that moment, Cecile opened the curtains to peer into the night. She saw Saint Nicholas whispering with his assistant Ruphrecht.

"Are you sure there is nothing left in the sacks?" asked Saint Nicholas.

"No, your Holiness, there's nothing. Why not promise Cecile that next year she'll get two or three times as many gifts?"

"Never, Ruphrecht, never," Saint Nicholas answered. "I cannot possibly disappoint Cecile."

Ruphrecht puffed on his pipe, deep in thought. "But Eminence, we don't have time to go back. The stores are empty, everyone is asleep, and moreover, we are forbidden to awaken anyone."

Cecile's heart almost stopped. Suddenly, she had an idea. She flung open the door. "Please, Saint Nicholas, not *everything* is sold. In Trinchen Mutser's shop there is a big chocolate boat, the *Congo*."

Saint Nicholas turned to Ruphrecht. "See, not *everything* is gone. To Trinchen Mutser's!" Then he remembered, "Ah, we are not allowed to awaken anybody."

"Can't *I* wake her up?" Cecile asked.

Saint Nicholas clapped his hands. "We are saved! On to The Sugared Nostril. Now."

Cecile led the way through the silent, snowy streets. In a corner window, Ruphrecht saw the

shadow of another person who was not asleep. The dark profile bobbed this way and that, its mouth moving all the time.

"A poet," Ruphrecht said, smiling.

When they arrived at The Sugared Nostril, Saint Nicholas urged, "Quickly, wake up Trinchen Mutser." Cecile beat her fists against the shop's door but made only a feeble sound.

"Louder," commanded Ruphrecht.

"If I knock any harder, it won't be any louder, believe me. I'm trying as hard as I can," said Cecile, almost in tears. And, even though the child knocked and kicked, Trinchen Mutser snored and snored.

"Ah, the shadow in the window!" Ruphrecht remembered. "He is not asleep. I will go fetch him."

"Of course, the poet," said Saint Nicholas. They rushed to the poet Remoldus Keersmacher's house. Ruphrecht shaped a snowball and aimed it at the window. The shadow paused, the window opened and the poet spoke into the night.

"Which muse is here to inspire me?"

"Me, Saint Nicholas," the bishop shouted. "You must awaken Trinchen Mutser, the shopkeeper," and he explained the problem.

"But are you the *real* Saint Nicholas?" Remoldus Keersmacher called down.

"Of course I am."

So the poet joined them, bowing and chattering about Dante, Homer, Virgil, Milton and the other poets he believed Saint Nicholas knew in Heaven. When they arrived at Trinchen Mutser's shop, Remoldus Keersmacher beat on the door with such a fervor that the shopkeeper jumped out of bed and rushed to the window.

"Is this the end of the world?" she yelled.

"We have come for the *Congo*..." Saint Nicholas started to explain. In a flash, Trinchen Mutser opened the door, turned up the lights and stood behind the counter ready to serve the unlikely group.

"He must be the bishop of Mechlin," she thought to herself. But aloud she said, "Your Excellency, the *Congo* is made from the finest chocolate. Just look at the cotton smoke, the gumdrops, mints, marzipan, biscuits and icing. All for fifty marks." Although the price was only forty marks, Trinchen Mutser thought a bishop could afford more.

Schokoladen-
schiff "Kongo"

The shopkeeper wanted money, but Saint Nicholas had none. Ruphrecht did not have any either, nor did the child or the poet. Each looked from one to the other.

"Do it for poetry's sake," pleaded Remoldus Keersmacher. But Trinchen Mutser did not budge.

"Do it for your own sake," said Ruphrecht. "Next

year I shall buy up your entire store." But even that promise did not sway Trinchen Mutser.

"Do it for God," urged Saint Nicholas.

"Do it, *please*," said Cecile.

Suddenly, thinking they might be a band of thieves, the shopkeeper screamed, "Get out. Holy Saint Anthony and Saint Nicholas, protect me."

"But I *am* Saint Nicholas," said the bishop.

"That's who you look like, but you don't have a groschen on you. You can't fool me. Out, or I shall get the watchman."

"Money destroys all brotherly love," said Saint Nicholas.

"It is money that destroys noble poetry," sighed Remoldus Keersmacher.

"...it's money that makes poor people poorer," Cecile thought.

"And, it can't make a chimney sweep clean," Ruphrecht chortled as he opened the door. Outside, in the calm night, they heard the song *Sleep Well* coming from a tower.

"Aha! Yet another person who does not sleep!" Saint Nicholas exclaimed.

"Keep the shopkeeper awake," called Ruphrecht over his shoulder as he raced to the tower. When he entered the tower room, the night watchman, Dries Andijvel, was playing the violin. Ruphrecht tried to win the watchman's attention. It was only when

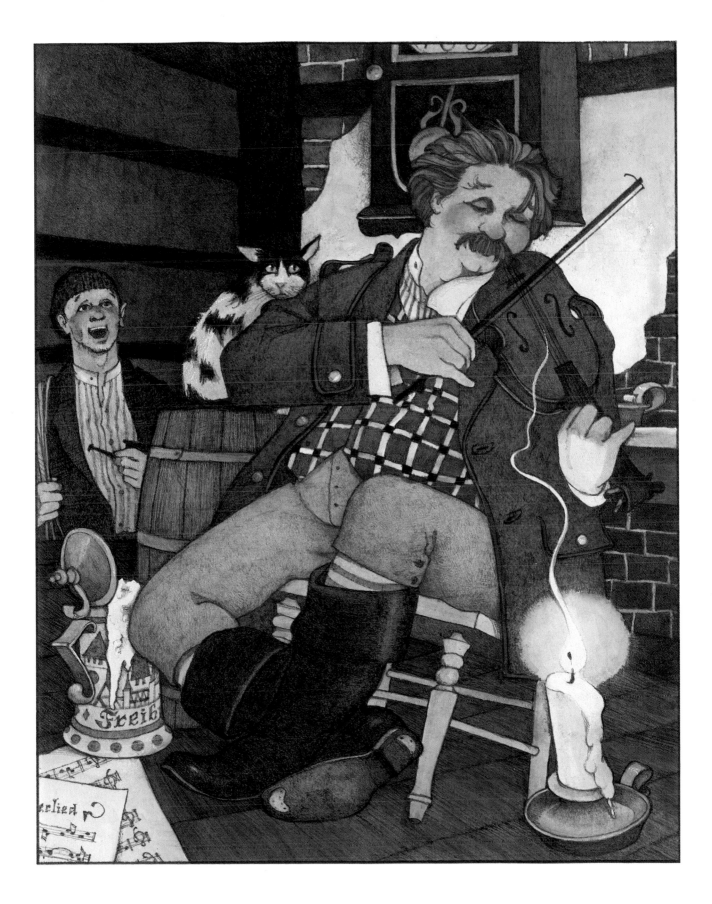

he seized the violin that Dries Andijvel stopped playing and listened to Ruphrecht's story.

Taking a long swallow on his beer, Dries Andijvel burped, "First I must zee to believe thizz craazzy tale." They stumbled down the stairs and on to The Sugared Nostril. When he saw the night watchman, Saint Nicholas begged him to pay the fifty marks, promising that if he agreed, all the luck in the world would be his. Though the man was touched, he confessed he had spent his last groschen on a keg of the darkest lager.

At her door, Trinchen Mutser insisted. "Fifty marks!"

Sighing, Saint Nicholas turned to Cecile. "Well, there is nothing more to be done. More than anything, I had hoped to see this woman, who is so hard of heart, give up her stingy ways, but it is not possible. Remember, there is always next year."

With a heavy sadness, Saint Nicholas looked one final time at Trinchen Mutser, then turned away. Ruphrecht paused just long enough to stare coldly into the shopkeeper's unyielding eyes.

One by one, the group left The Sugared Nostril. The poet returned to his poetry, the night watchman to his tower and Cecile to her dreams. Saint Nicholas and Ruphrecht gathered up their empty sacks.

Trinchen Mutser trundled off to bed, still worrying about the unsold *Congo*. She moved from window to window, checking the curtains one more time. As she reached the very last one, bright moonlight filled her shop, and peeking around the curtain, Trinchen Mutser saw a donkey soaring into the sky. A flash of rainbow colored the town.

"What? I must be wearier than I ever imagined. No...it couldn't be...Was it really him?" she gasped, rubbing her eyes. "It...I have been a fool, an old, old fool. Of course, that kind man *is* Saint Nicholas, the bishop. Poor little Cecile." Clutching at her sweater, she ran through her shop, grabbing the beautiful chocolate *Congo*.

When the dazzling moonlight faded into a quiet dawn, Cecile awakened. Through tearstained eyes she saw the *Congo*. Her heart pounded. It was there, after all, puffing its ninety groschen of cotton smoke, nestled on the cold hearth. How was it possible? How?

Well, no one knows for sure—neither the shopkeeper, the poet, the night watchman, the kind bishop nor his skillful assistant. No one will ever tell the secret of how the chocolate *Congo* came to the child Cecile.

Saint Nicholas was a real person who lived in Asia Minor more than fifteen hundred years ago. While a bishop, he performed many good deeds—from rescuing shipwrecked sailors, to delivering three penniless women from slavery, to saving two young students from cannibalism. He became the patron saint of Greece, Sicily, Norway and Russia, where five czars were named after him.

Saint Nicholas Eve is celebrated in Europe on December 5, the anniversary of the bishop's death in A.D. 343. There are countless legends about how Saint Nicholas returns each year, while everyone is soundly asleep, to leave gifts for well-behaved children. In one story, he arrives in a boat from Spain with a moor as his sidekick. In other accounts, he visits on a donkey with his assistant, a chimney sweep.

In some countries, children leave carrots and apples for Saint Nicholas's donkey and their shoes by the door for the bishop to fill with gifts. Some legends describe how treats descend from the chimney or fly through the door.

A Gift from Saint Nicholas has been freely adapted for an English-speaking audience from an original story, *St. Nicholas in Nood*, by Felix Timmermans, a Flemish artist and author who created books for children that have been translated throughout the world.

Thanks to Despina Croussouloudis for catching my publisher's ear and to Marianne Carus, for telling me about Freiburg im Breisgau.
C.M.